End Game

Paul Blum

RISING STARS

nasen
Helping Everyone Achieve

NASEN House, 4/5 Amber Business Village, Amber Close,
Amington, Tamworth, Staffordshire, B77 4RP

Rising Stars UK Ltd.
7 Hatchers Mews, Bermondsey Street, London SE1 3GS
www.risingstars-uk.com

Published 2012

Cover design: Burville-Riley Partnership
Brighton photographs: iStock
Illustrations: Chris King for Illustration Ltd (characters and cover artwork)/
Abigail Daker (map) http://illustratedmaps.info
Text design and typesetting: Geoff Rayner
Publisher: Rebecca Law
Editorial manager: Sasha Morton Creative Project Management

British Library Cataloguing in Publication Data.
A CIP record for this book is available from the British Library.

ISBN: 978-0-85769-604-5

Printed and bound by CPI Group (UK) Ltd, Croydon, CR0 4YY

MIX
Paper from
responsible sources
FSC
www.fsc.org   FSC® C020471

Contents

Name:
John Logan

Age:
24

Hometown:
Manchester

Occupation:
Author of
supernatural
thrillers

Special skills:
Not yet known

profiles

Name:
Rose Petal

Age:
22

Hometown:
Brighton

Occupation:
Yoga teacher,
nightclub and
shop owner,
vampire hunter

Special skills:
Private investigator
specialising in
supernatural
crime

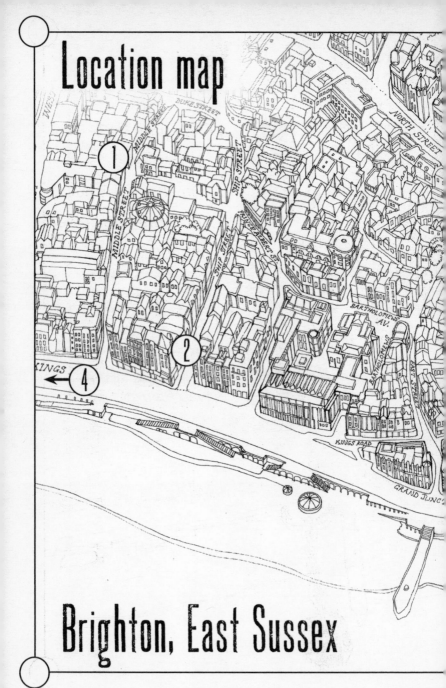

Location map

Brighton, East Sussex

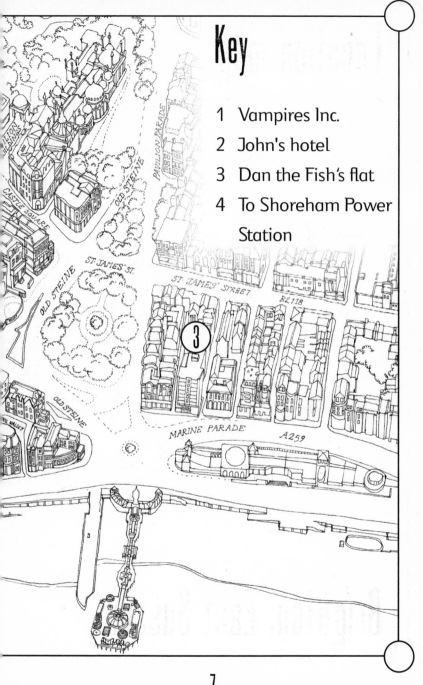

Key

1 Vampires Inc.
2 John's hotel
3 Dan the Fish's flat
4 To Shoreham Power Station

Chapter 1

John Logan liked sunrise in Brighton best. He loved watching the sun coming up over the sea and bringing a new day. John was an author and Rose Petal was helping him to research his second book. Rose owned a nightclub called Vampires Inc. and a shop. During the few months he had been in Brighton, he had found out that supernatural creatures really did exist. Rose worked as an investigator, solving vampire-related crimes. While he had been working alongside her, John had come across werewolves and shape-shifting demons, too. Now he had enough information to go home and write his book.

John packed up his things slowly. He was going to miss Brighton and he was really going to miss Rose. When he had checked out of his hotel room, John's last stop before getting the train home was to Vampires Inc. – it was time to say goodbye.

Rose was sitting at her laptop when John arrived at the club. She looked happy to see him.

'I realised something, John. We can carry on working together even when you are in Manchester!' she said. 'I've linked up our two computers. From there, you can access all my contacts and files. I've even given you a database of all the friendly local vampires so you can ask them for tips when you are writing. See!'

Rose opened up a file and clicked through it. In his bag, John's own laptop beeped. He laughed. 'Rose, you are as good with computers as you are with vampires!' He ruffled Rose's spiky red hair and gave her a hug. 'I really am going to miss you.'

'I'm going to miss you too,' thought Rose as she hugged John back. She didn't notice a hidden camera behind John that was recording their every word.

★★★★

'We have found a database of Brighton's vampires,' hissed a voice minutes later. 'Yes, we can get it for you. But the price will be high.'

On the other end of the telephone, a man spoke. 'No price is too high. The Ace of Spades project still needs a few more subjects for a live test. We just need to know where the last few vampires live.' There was a click and the line went dead.

The shape-shifters looked at each other. They had pleased their leader, and they had found the one man who had seen them change shape and lived to tell the tale. They were going to enjoy killing John Logan. He had escaped from them once. It would not happen again.

Chapter 2

'John, I've got one more job I need your help with before you go back to Manchester,' said Rose. 'I want to check the information on this database. Are any vampires missing? Has anybody moved in or out of Brighton in the last few months? There's a guy who we can ask, but he's a bit odd.'

'I'm used to people here being odd now,' said John.

'Then you'll enjoy meeting Dan the Fish,' grinned Rose.

That afternoon, Rose and John went to visit Dan the Fish. He was an elderly vampire and so large that it took him a long time to get down the stairs to open his front door.

'Dan, don't breathe on us,' said Rose as they entered his small flat.

'I haven't been up to anything, Rose. I promise,' Dan replied. But his breath smelled so strongly of fish that Logan had to take a step back and hold his nose.

'Dan, what did I tell you about stealing fish?' said Rose crossly. 'You're frightening the humans in the park. Standing in the pond biting the heads off the goldfish is not on.'

'It's just so hard being a vampire in Brighton,' said Dan. 'Humans are off the menu, I get into trouble when I steal cats and dogs and the rats are too fast for me to catch. I like fish because they are so salty.'

John tried not to laugh. Dan the Fish looked very sorry for himself.

'I know it's wrong,' said Dan. 'I never wanted to do it, but I've been so nervous since they locked me up.'

'Who locked you up?' asked Rose.

'I don't know who they were. But they put me in a cage,' he replied. 'They fed me blood. They tried to make me fight and kill other creatures. I was too old and fat, so in the end, they let me go.'

'Dan, have you heard of the Ace of Spades project?' asked John.

He nodded slowly. 'Yes, I have. They

gave me drugs to make me forget what I'd seen there, but they didn't work on me. My stomach can absorb anything. So I can remember all the things that happened. It was really bad, Rose. No wonder a lot of the local vampires are leaving town.'

Most supernatural beings in Brighton knew about the Ace of Spades project and feared it. It was supposed to be top secret, but Rose and John had come across it before. Rose believed that vampires on the project were being trained to kill in new and savage ways.

'Do you know where they kept you?' asked Rose.

Dan showed her a fishy-smelling map he had printed out. 'I was blindfolded, so I might be wrong. But I think this is it.'

'That looks like Shoreham Power Station,' she said. 'It's not far from Brighton. We should check it out.'

Logan agreed. They left Dan with a printout of the vampire database. Dan agreed to update it with the names of the vampires who were still in Brighton and email it back to John. Then Rose and John headed back to the club. John had become too interested in the Ace of Spades project to go home now.

A few hours later, John had fallen asleep on Rose's sofa. He had left his laptop on. A new email pinged in from Dan. It contained the updated vampire database. A minute after that, the computer beeped again. The file had been downloaded by someone and deleted from John's inbox. In the corner of the room, a camera whirred … Somebody was watching everything.

Chapter 3

Shoreham Power Station was by the
sea. An eerie red light shone out of the
chimney over the water. It was a windy
night and the sea was high. The waves
were crashing down on the rocks. John
and Rose were parked nearby in their
friend Rodney's car.

'The boats down there must bring in
coal for the power station,' said John,
looking at the harbour through his
binoculars.

'Or vampires in cages for the Ace of
Spades project,' said Rose.

John nodded. 'Nobody would see

or hear a thing out here. It's a great location for a secret!'

Nobody was on guard at the power station, as they climbed the fence. There were lots of old buildings. All of them looked dark and empty. They carried on walking. Rose Petal shone her torch on the map. 'I think this must be it,' she said. She started walking on ahead. 'Plant A. It was shut down thirty years ago.'

Suddenly, Logan pulled Rose back. 'Listen,' he said in a whisper. 'Can you hear something? I think it's coming from Plant A.'

He was right. The sound of screaming rose above the howling wind and noisy sea. They tried the door but it was locked. Rose shone her torch in through the window.

'Oh no!' gasped Rose.

Rows and rows of cages held vampires. Rose recognised some of them from the club. There were bruises on their faces and hands. Their teeth had grown extra long and dripped blood. Their eyes looked blank as they scratched at the bars of their prisons. There were other captives in the dark room that howled like wolves.

'Welcome to the Ace of Spades,' said Logan, shivering. In the darkness, neither of them saw the shape-shifters lurking. They were following John Logan. When the time was right, they would strike.

Rose Petal made two phone calls when they got back to the car. First of all, she phoned her old boyfriend, Alex Reddy. Alex was a powerful vampire from the family of Elders. He was the lead singer with a band called The Night Killers. All of his bandmates were vampires.

Next, Rose called Rob Robson, the leader of the Lukos Chapter. This gang of werewolves hated Alex but had helped Rose before. If werewolves were in danger they would want to know. Rose told both men the same thing — that she needed them to bring their boys to Vampires Inc. straight away.

****

John watched as Alex Reddy and his band of vampires arrived outside the club. The band rode sleek motor scooters. Alex's silver scooter was polished and gleaming. It seemed to fly just above the ground. John rolled his eyes.

Five minutes later, Rob Robson and his werewolf biker gang pulled up on their big motorbikes. Usually when The Night Killers and the Lukos Chapter met, it was to fight. Tonight, they were on the same side.

Rose showed Rob and Alex a map of Shoreham Power Station. Alex had arranged for two of his tour lorries to be used. They would transport the drugged prisoners to safety tomorrow night.

The vampires would be taken to a secret location where the Elders would help them recover. Rob would use the other lorry to take the werewolf prisoners into hiding. While all the planning was taking place, John checked his emails.

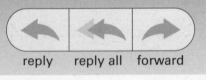

reply   reply all   forward

From: Dan-the-Fish@dannet.uk

To: John Logan, Writer

Subject: Vampire database

John, hope you got the updated database file. Not many of us left. I'm leaving town for a while. I heard a rumour that it's going to get dangerous here.

Take care.

Dan

Just then, the email moved itself to the deleted items. John tried to find the message but it was gone. He looked at his inbox again. There was no database from Dan. The laptop suddenly started to beep and a tiny icon in the corner flashed. It said 'Start remote back-up'. Suddenly, John knew that his computer was being hacked! He quickly turned the power off and looked around the room.

Meanwhile, the vampires and werewolves were talking rather than fighting. It felt odd for both groups.

'We've been looking for some missing wolves over the last few weeks,' said Rob to Alex. 'They must be taking our kind as well as yours.'

'More vampires went missing tonight,' Alex replied. 'This is getting serious for both of us.'

Rose was watching John as he climbed onto a chair. He was peering at the security camera. 'John, what are you doing?' she asked.

'Shh,' said John quietly. He lifted the camera down and took off the back. A mile down the road, a screen in a room went blank. The shape-shifters started to pack up their gear. Their enemy, John Logan, had just found out the club was bugged. It was time for them to leave.

'Get the cameras down,' said John to Rob and Alex, who found secret listening devices inside them. John told them about his laptop being hacked.

The names of Brighton's vampires were on the stolen database. The Ace of Spades project had found them.

Rob smashed the cameras on the floor. 'So, whoever runs the project must know our plan by now,' he said angrily. Alex thought fast. He could get the lorries to meet them at the power station that night. They needed to free the prisoners twenty-four hours earlier than planned. Rob and his wolf gang agreed. They needed to surprise the leaders of the project. It had to be tonight.

31

Chapter 4

John jumped onto the back of Rob's
bike. He hoped that he would survive
the night. This adventure would
make an amazing plot for his book.
The speed with which the werewolf
bikes travelled along the coast took
his breath away. Yet, he still noticed a
strange flash of silver on the water as
they got closer to the power station.
He had seen that happen once before
– on the night a pair of demon shape-
shifters had tried to kill him.

   It was quiet when they arrived at the
power station. John told Rose and Rob

about the flash of silver in the water. It was possible the shape-shifters had got there before them. Five minutes later, the boys from The Night Killers pulled up on their scooters. Under their long coats, they had an array of weapons. The vampires were prepared for anything. The battle was on.

There were still no signs of life as Rose and John led their team to Plant A. But as they got closer, they began to hear screams and howls. Then John stopped and pointed to the floor. He was standing in a puddle that hadn't been there a moment ago. Looking round, he saw a flash of silver again. The shape-shifters travelled by water! John heard a voice hiss, 'Logan!'

'Demons!' yelled John but his warning came too late. Six snarling shape-shifters jumped out of the darkness. The Lukos Chapter swiftly changed into werewolves. The vampires bared their fangs. The shrieking vampires bit hard and deep, and the wolves slashed with their claws. The shape-shifters tore flesh and bone with their long talons. The battle was violent and deadly.

Rose and John were carrying flame-throwers. They hid behind a low wall and took aim. Rob roared orders at his gang. The wolves pushed the demons back into one place to give Rose and John a clear shot. Alex was there to give some extra help. He drove his silver scooter right at the demons. Hidden in its gleaming headlights was a laser which he used to kill two of the demons. He burned a ring into the ground around the rest. They had become a glowing target!

'Now!' yelled Alex.

John and Rose pointed the flame-throwers and fired. The shape-shifters screeched and their long, pointed tails thrashed around. They could not survive the burning flames for long. Within moments, their scales exploded and they were gone. Rose shouted out in triumph and threw her arms around John. Alex looked on with a sad smile. He knew Rose's heart no longer belonged to him.

The vampires and werewolves ran past the burning demons and freed the project's prisoners. The frightened guards had already run away just as Alex's lorries pulled up. They loaded up the freed vampires and werewolves, and drove off into the night. The Ace of Spades project was over.

Chapter 5

A week later, at Vampires Inc., Rose and John held a party. Alex Reddy and Rob Robson brought their boys, family and friends. For the first time in the club's history, it was full of vampires and werewolves but there was no fighting. At midnight, Rose turned off the music and made a speech.

'I want to thank everyone, whether you are human, vampire or werewolf. Someone tried to destroy our supernatural community,' she shouted into the microphone. 'We have always lived in freedom in this wonderful city.

Thanks to all of you, it can stay that way for a little while longer!'

Everybody cheered. Rose leapt back down from the stage and into John's arms. There was a wolf whistle from one of the wolves. Everybody laughed as Rose blushed and John smiled. He was very proud of his girlfriend!

Rob and Alex had a lot to talk about. The vampires and werewolves they had freed from the Ace of Spades project were getting their strength back with every day. Soon, most of them would return to Brighton. They would also be able to explain what they had been training for. There had indeed been a plan to wage a war on humans. For now, that threat was gone.

The next morning, John Logan and Rose Petal walked along the beach. It was early morning, John's favourite time of day.

The sun was just coming up over the sea. The beach was empty. They had the beginning of the day all to themselves.

'I'm so pleased you're staying here,' Rose said to John.

'Now that no one is trying to kill me I can get on with writing my book!' he joked. He hugged Rose. 'I think I should be living near to my assistant. Just in case I need some more help with my research.'

'Do you think I'm still the right girl for the job?' asked Rose, looking into his eyes.

'You're definitely the right girl for the job,' smiled John. 'And you're the right girl for me as well.' John took Rose's hand in his and together they walked to the edge of the waves. It felt like it was going to be a great day.

Glossary

array — a variety or mixture

bared their fangs — showed their vampire teeth

flame-thrower — a long thin tube that shoots out fire

listening devices — hidden microphones that secretly record voices

power station — a big building which makes electricity by burning coal or gas

shape-shifter — a supernatural creature that can change its shape and appearance in a split second

wolf whistle — when a person whistles at another person to say 'You are looking good!'

Quiz

1   What time of day in Brighton does John Logan like best?

2   What does John Logan intend to do when he returns to Manchester?

3   Why are the shape-shifting demons watching Vampires Inc. on a secret camera?

4   Why is one vampire named Dan the Fish?

5   What is being done to vampires and werewolves on the Ace of Spades project?

6   Who wants to kill John Logan?

7   Who does Rose Petal turn to for help?

8   How do Rose and John kill the shape-shifting demons?

9   What colour is Alex Reddy's motor scooter?

10 Why doesn't John Logan go back to Manchester at the end of the story?

Quiz answers

1 Sunrise

2 Write his second book about vampires

3 They want to find the names of every last vampire in Brighton

4 He eats fish in the pond in the park every day

5 They are put in cages and made to fight and kill other creatures

6 The shape-shifters he had escaped from before

7 Alex Reddy and Rob Robson

8 They use flame-throwers

9 Silver

10 He has fallen in love with Rose and is going to stay with her in Brighton

About the author

The author of these books teaches in a London school. At the weekend, his research takes him to the beaches and back streets of Brighton in search of werewolves and vampires.

He writes about what he has found.